SHADOWS

OF THE

SPLIT

**"A Love Bound by Secrets, a City
Haunted by Death"**

garvita

To dreamers,
'khwab dekho, pure hote hain'
And future achievers,
'bahut dur aa gaye ho, dhyan rakho- apna
aur apno ka'

<u>**Appendix**</u>

**_Understanding the Key Themes of
Shadows of the Split_**

In Shadows of the Split, the
protagonist grapples with the
complex and often misunderstood
nature of the human mind,
particularly through the lens of
dissociative identity disorder (DID).
Through his journey, I sought to
explore themes of identity,
psychological fragmentation, and
absurdism, which are central not
only to the narrative but also to the
broader philosophical and
psychological ideas that have
inspired this work. In this appendix,

I'll break down these key themes in more detail, providing readers with a deeper understanding of the conditions and philosophies that shape the story.

1. Dissociative Identity Disorder (DID)

Dissociative Identity Disorder, once known as multiple personality disorder, is a mental health condition in which an individual experiences two or more distinct identities or personality states. These identities, or "alters," often have different names, characteristics, and behaviors, and may not be aware of each other's existence. DID is typically a result of severe trauma, particularly during early childhood, and is a coping mechanism for individuals who have endured overwhelming abuse or neglect.

In Shadows of the Split, the protagonist suffers from DID without initially realizing it, which creates a compelling and disturbing dynamic within the narrative. The condition manifests itself as a split between the officer's primary identity and an alternate persona that emerges in moments of stress or conflict. The officer is both the investigator trying to solve a series of murders and, unbeknownst to him, the killer committing them. This duality becomes the heart of the psychological thriller, where the protagonist's search for self-awareness mirrors his unraveling sense of control over his own mind.

The Origins of DID:

DID is often linked to severe trauma, particularly in early childhood. This trauma could be physical, emotional, or sexual abuse, or prolonged exposure to an environment of neglect or abandonment. The mind's response to this trauma is often to dissociate, meaning that the person detaches from the full experience of their feelings and memories. Over time, this dissociation can develop into the creation of separate identities as a way to compartmentalize the overwhelming emotions or memories. These identities may emerge at different times, often in response to specific triggers, and may have their own distinct traits, memories, and behaviors.

In the case of the protagonist in Shadows of the Split, his identity disorder is rooted in his past experiences—memories that he can't *fully access or comprehend until the investigation forces him to confront them. His alternating personalities serve as both a coping mechanism and a source of chaos, which amplifies the tension and mystery within the narrative.*

Treatment of DID:

While there is no singular "cure" for DID, therapy, particularly a specialized form of psychotherapy called "integrative therapy," is used to help individuals integrate their different identities and regain a cohesive sense of self. Treatment often involves long-term therapeutic work, aimed at addressing the underlying trauma and helping the person develop healthier coping mechanisms.

In the story, the protagonist's inability to fully integrate his alters creates a sense of fragmentation that drives the plot forward. His struggle *for self-understanding parallels the psychological battle many individuals with DID face in real life—an ongoing process of reintegrating the different facets of their identity while grappling with the emotional pain of past trauma.*

2. Absurdism and the Meaning of Life

Absurdism is a philosophical perspective that was popularized by thinkers like Albert Camus, who argued that life's inherent lack of meaning leads to a sense of absurdity. According to absurdism, humans search for meaning and order in a chaotic, indifferent universe, but are often confronted with the realization that such meaning is elusive. This confrontation with the absurd leads to what Camus calls "the absurd hero"—an individual who refuses to surrender to despair despite the lack of meaning in life.

In Shadows of the Split, absurdism serves as a central philosophical theme, influencing both the psychological condition of the protagonist and the overarching narrative. The officer's identity disorder is a metaphor for the absurdity of human existence—the fragmentation of the self, the search for meaning in a chaotic world, and *the inability to fully comprehend the forces shaping one's actions.*

The Absurd Hero:

The protagonist's journey can be interpreted as a reflection of the absurd hero, as described by Camus. Throughout the book, the officer strives to make sense of the murders he is investigating, only to find that his own fractured psyche is the very source of the violence. His refusal to accept the absurdity of his condition and his determination to uncover the truth parallels Camus' notion of the absurd hero who continues to fight against the indifference of the universe.

The officer's actions, although motivated by a desire for justice, are ultimately futile in the face of the larger existential questions he is confronting. His inability to reconcile his fragmented identities symbolizes the futility of seeking absolute meaning in a world that resists such clarity. Like Camus' Sisyphus, who is condemned to roll a boulder up a hill only for it to roll back down again, the officer is caught in a never-ending cycle of investigation and violence, trapped by the absurdity of his own condition.

The Search for Meaning:

Throughout the book, the officer grapples with his quest for meaning—both in his investigation and in his life. As he uncovers more about the murders and his own psyche, he is forced to confront the possibility that there may be no inherent meaning to either his actions or his existence. This confrontation with meaninglessness is at the heart of the book's psychological tension, as the officer's unraveling self-awareness mirrors the broader human condition of searching for meaning in a meaningless world.

Absurdism, then, offers a lens through which to understand the protagonist's struggle. The meaning of the murders, and indeed the meaning of the officer's life, remains elusive, suggesting that perhaps the only resolution is to embrace the absurdity and continue the search, even without the hope of finding answers.

3. Psychological Exploration of Identity

A central theme of Shadows of the Split is the exploration of identity. The protagonist's dissociative identity disorder is a manifestation of the complexities and fractures within the self. Identity is not a fixed, unchanging entity, but rather something fluid, shaped by experiences, memories, and emotions. The protagonist's struggle to reconcile his different identities highlights the malleable and often contradictory nature of identity, and the difficulty of truly understanding who we are.

The Fractured Self:

The notion of a fractured self is explored in depth throughout the book. The protagonist is not a singular, cohesive person, but rather a collection of different selves that are at odds with each other. This fragmentation creates a sense of alienation and confusion, as the officer is forced to live with the knowledge that he is both the investigator and the criminal, both the hero and the villain.

In many ways, this internal fragmentation mirrors the broader human experience of grappling with contradictory impulses and desires.

We are not always consistent in our thoughts, actions, and emotions, and the fragmentation of the officer's identity serves as a metaphor for the way in which our sense of self can be fractured by internal conflict.

The Search for Self-Understanding:

As the officer unravels the mystery of the murders and his own identity, he embarks on a journey of self-discovery. The psychological tension in the book arises from the officer's inability to fully understand who he is, and from the realization that his identity is not something fixed or stable, but rather something fluid and subject to change. This uncertainty about the self is a central theme of the book, reflecting the difficulty we all face in understanding our true nature.

In this sense, Shadows of the Split is as much about the search for self-awareness as it is about solving a crime. The officer's investigation into the murders becomes intertwined with his investigation into his own mind, as he seeks to understand the forces that have shaped him and the identities he inhabits.

Conclusion

The themes of dissociative identity disorder, absurdism, and identity exploration in Shadows of the Split are central not only to the story but also to the deeper philosophical and psychological questions that the book raises. Through the protagonist's journey, I have sought to explore the complexities of the human mind, the search for meaning in a chaotic world, and the fractured nature of identity. These themes are not only key to understanding the book but also reflect the broader questions that we all confront as we navigate the complexities of life and the human condition.

Author's Note

Dear Reader,

From the bottom of my heart, thank you for picking up this book. Writing this story has been an unforgettable journey—one filled with late-night ideas, endless cups of chai, and a deep dive into the human psyche. To know that you've joined me on this journey means the world.

I have always been fascinated by the complexities of human nature, the blurred lines between good and evil, and the chaos that shapes us. As a student of Physics, Chemistry, and Mathematics, I love seeking patterns in the universe, but in storytelling, I embrace the unpredictable. Through my writing, I explore the depths of identity, morality, and the absurd beauty of life itself.

This book wouldn't exist without the people who have supported me—my father, my mother, and my sister for listening to me rant about how much my back and shoulders hurt while working on this, my friends, and every single person who has ever believed in my words. And most importantly, you, dear reader. Whether this book made you think, feel, or simply kept you turning the pages, I am endlessly grateful.

Here's to stories that challenge,
inspire, and linger long after they
end.

With gratitude,
 Garvita Suyal

Chapter 1

Somewhere in the quaint city of Bangalore, Karnataka, in the year 1998, the cries of a newborn echoed through the sterile halls of Jaishankar Hospital. The sound was pure and piercing, a harbinger of new life.

"Congratulations, Mr. Patil! You are blessed with a baby boy. You may now see your wife and child," the nurse said with a warm smile, her voice soft yet brimming with pride. She excused herself, briskly heading toward the reception to finalize receipts and documents, leaving Mr. Patil standing in the hospital lobby, his heart pounding with a mixture of joy and relief.

Tears welled up in his eyes—tears of profound joy that blurred the deep sorrow he had carried for three long years since the loss of his firstborn. The wound of that heartbreak had left an indelible scar, but today, the heavens seemed to grant him and his wife a second chance. Overcome with emotion, he sprinted down the hall toward the operation theater, his footsteps echoing against the cold marble floors.

As he entered the room, his gaze fell upon his wife, pale but glowing with maternal warmth. Kneeling beside her bed, he gently clasped her hand, kissing it tenderly—a silent but heartfelt gesture of gratitude and love. His trembling hands reached out to cradle the infant swaddled in soft white cloth. The moment he held his son, a wave of emotion surged through him, a powerful sensation he hadn't felt since three years ago, when life had cruelly snatched his first child away.

Before he could fully savor the joy, the room erupted with jubilant cries—relatives, brimming with excitement, had arrived to celebrate the birth. Their laughter and cheers filled the small space with energy, but amidst the chaos, tragedy almost struck.

Distracted by the commotion, Mr. Patil's grip faltered. In an instant, the infant slipped from his hands, landing on the bed beside his mother. A sickening thud followed as the baby's tiny head grazed the wooden edge of the cot. The room fell deathly silent, the joyous cries replaced by gasps of horror.

The infant's shrill wails pierced the air as panic gripped the room. Nurses and doctors rushed in, summoned by Mr. Patil's desperate shouts. Time seemed to stretch unbearably as they examined the baby, their hushed whispers intensifying the parents' fear. After a few tense moments, a doctor finally turned to the couple, her expression calm yet reassuring.

"The baby is perfectly fine," she said, her voice steady. "No need to worry, Mr. Patil."

Relief washed over Mrs. Patil, and her trembling hands reached for her child. She drew the baby close, her tears of anxiety replaced by tears of gratitude. Holding her son tightly, she pressed a gentle kiss to his soft, tiny forehead.

"Atharva," she whispered, her voice filled with love and determination. "I'll name him Atharva."

The days that followed were a whirlwind of diapers, late-night feedings, and quiet moments of wonder. Little Atharva quickly became the light of the Patil household. His wide, curious eyes followed his parents everywhere, his laughter filling the house with a warmth they hadn't felt in years.

As Atharva began to crawl, his adventurous spirit revealed itself. One morning, while Mrs. Patil was folding laundry, she turned to find Atharva crawling toward the edge of the bed. Her heart leapt as he tumbled off, but a pile of soft pillows broke his fall. His reaction? A hearty giggle that left his mother shaking her head in amused disbelief.

Then there was the time Mr. Patil decided to introduce Atharva to the family dog, Raja, a gentle Labrador with a fondness for licking faces. The moment Atharva reached out his chubby hands, Raja responded with an enthusiastic lick, toppling the baby backward. Atharva's head bumped against the floor, but once again, his cries turned to laughter as his father scooped him up and kissed his forehead.

"He's made of steel, this one," Mr. Patil joked, though he made a mental note to be more careful.

As Atharva grew, his mischievous streak only deepened. At 18 months, he loved chasing butterflies in the garden, often stumbling and bumping into flower pots, much to his parents' exasperation. Yet, no matter how many times he fell, Atharva always got back up, his determination shining through even in these small moments.

One evening, as the family gathered for dinner, Atharva took his first wobbly steps. His mother gasped, dropping her spoon, while his father rushed forward, arms outstretched, ready to catch him if he fell. The toddler's triumphant grin was met with cheers, and for the Patils, it was yet another reminder of the resilience and joy their little boy brought into their lives.

Through every bump and stumble, Atharva's journey was a testament to life's delicate balance of joy and fear, laughter and tears. And though no one could predict the twists and turns that lay ahead, one thing was certain: Atharva was destined to leave an indelible mark on the world around him.

Chapter 2

Twenty-five years later, Atharva had become a man of remarkable stature. From the baby who had once fought for his life, he had risen to embody strength and resolve in every aspect of his being. Now a seasoned police officer, his reputation was one of unmatched excellence. With his sharp mind and unyielding determination, Atharva had swiftly climbed the ranks, securing not only the admiration of his peers but the undivided respect of the entire nation.

His name echoed in every corner of the city, synonymous with justice. At the age of 28, his cold demeanor and unwavering commitment had earned him a reputation that few could rival. He was known for being calculated, always several steps ahead of his enemies, yet beneath the hard exterior lay a softer side—one that only a select few ever glimpsed. His ability to stay calm under pressure, to analyze and solve cases with an almost supernatural precision, made him a force to be reckoned with.

In his three years of service, not a single case had slipped through his fingers. Murders, kidnappings, smuggling operations—Atharva dismantled them all with surgical efficiency. Every challenge was met with a clear strategy and an unshakeable resolve. His colleagues marveled at his brilliance, while criminals feared his name, knowing that evading him was an impossible task. It wasn't just his intellect that made him successful—it was his unwavering moral compass and his commitment to serving the public that set him apart.

Children idolized him, seeing him as a hero who could vanquish evil with a mere glance. His story of overcoming tragedy, of rising from the ashes of his own loss, inspired countless young minds to follow the path of righteousness. In classrooms across the city, teachers spoke of him with admiration, sharing the story of a boy who grew into a man of indomitable will. Some even wore his image as a badge of hope, a reminder that no adversity was too great to overcome.

Atharva's extraordinary accomplishments did not go unnoticed. The nation celebrated his unparalleled service, and it was no surprise when he was awarded the prestigious **Ashoka Chakra**, a symbol of valor and sacrifice. The ceremony was a moment of triumph—not just for Atharva, but for his parents, who watched with pride and tears in their eyes as their son stood tall, a shining beacon of resilience. His mother, now older but still filled with the same maternal warmth, couldn't help but recall the fragile infant she had once cradled, and the countless prayers she had whispered over him.

But Atharva's journey was far from over. His work had caught the attention of higher authorities, and his transfer to a prominent post in the capital was a testament to his rising influence. This new chapter promised broader responsibilities and the opportunity to shape the justice system in ways he had only dreamed of.

As he packed his belongings, ready to leave behind his familiar precinct,

Atharva found himself reflecting on the countless lives he had touched. He remembered the tearful gratitude of a mother whose kidnapped daughter he had rescued, the silent nods of respect from colleagues who had doubted him at first, and even the sneering criminals who ultimately confessed under the weight of his relentless pursuit.

Yet, Atharva wasn't one to bask in glory for long. Each victory only fueled his hunger to do more, to be better, to bring light to the darkest corners of the nation. And though he carried the weight of the world on his shoulders, he bore it with grace, his steps steady, his resolve unshaken.

As he stepped into his new role, Atharva was already a legend in the making, a man whose deeds would be etched in the annals of history. But even as the world celebrated his rise, the shadows of an unseen storm began to gather. For all his strength and resolve, Atharva was yet to face the one case that would test not just his skills, but the very core of his humanity.

Chapter 3

After ten years of dedicated service in the field, Atharva was transferred to Delhi, a city bustling with chaos and opportunity. The transfer came with the highest position in the force, a role that symbolized not just his professional excellence but also the trust placed in him to oversee justice in one of the most demanding cities in the nation. His life seemed to have reached a pinnacle of stability and purpose.

But stability is often fleeting.

One crisp December morning, as the city hummed to life outside his bungalow in South Delhi, Atharva's phone buzzed incessantly. Groggily, he reached for it, answering the call with his usual sharp tone.

"Sir, there's been a murder," came the voice of his subordinate.

"Murder?" Atharva sat up, his senses sharpening. It wasn't an unusual occurrence in a sprawling metropolis like Delhi, but something in the officer's voice unsettled him.

"It's... unusual, sir. A beggar. No known identity, no money, nothing to indicate why someone would go to the trouble of killing him."

Atharva's brow furrowed. "Send me the location."

Minutes later, dressed in his neatly pressed uniform, Atharva arrived at the scene—a dimly lit alley near **Chandni Chowk**, where the chaos of Delhi's crowded bazaars gave way to dark corners often forgotten by society. The body lay sprawled on the ground, covered with a tattered shawl, the man's gaunt face frozen in an expression of terror. Blood pooled beneath him, and from the position of the body, it was clear that the attack had been both brutal and deliberate.

He crouched near the body, studying the scene with meticulous care. There were no obvious clues—no footprints, no murder weapon, no personal belongings. It was as though the killer had melted into thin air.

"Why a beggar?" he murmured to himself. "No money, no background, no connections. What motive could there be?"

Atharva's mind churned with possibilities, but none seemed plausible. By the time he returned to his bungalow late that evening, his head throbbed with an intensity that made it hard to think. He poured himself a strong coffee, took a cold shower to clear his mind, and collapsed into bed, determined to tackle the mystery with fresh eyes in the morning.

But when morning came, the city delivered another shock.

"Another murder, sir," the same subordinate informed him. "This time, it's a rich CEO. Same pattern—no clear motive, no evidence."

Atharva's grip on the phone tightened. He rushed to the scene, finding the body of the CEO sprawled in his luxurious penthouse. The contrast between the two victims—the penniless beggar and the wealthy executive—was stark. It left Atharva baffled.

The murders didn't stop.

On the third day, a five-year-old child was killed, her small frame discovered in a park near **Hauz Khas Village**. The following day, an 89-year-old woman was found lifeless in her modest home in **Dwarka**, her wrinkled hands still clutching a prayer book.

Each morning brought fresh horror. For eight consecutive days, Delhi woke to news of another murder, each victim vastly different in age, social status, and background. There was no discernible pattern—no connection between the victims, no commonality in the method of killing, no logical sequence.

Atharva's once-sharp mind, known for its ability to decipher the most cryptic cases, was now clouded with frustration. The randomness of the killings was maddening, and the killer's ability to evade detection only deepened his unease.

Late one evening, as he sat in his study, surrounded by crime scene photos and notes, he ran his hands through his hair, his fingers gripping the roots as if trying to physically extract an answer.

"The beggar, the CEO, the child, the old woman... What am I missing?" he muttered aloud.

His bungalow, usually a sanctuary of calm, now felt suffocating. The walls seemed to close in as the weight of his responsibility pressed down on him. Every night, he braced himself for the phone call that would announce the next victim, and every night, he felt more powerless to prevent it.

The city's unease was palpable. News channels ran sensational headlines, demanding answers. The public grew restless, their trust in the police eroding with each passing day. And while Atharva's exterior remained cold and composed, inside, he was unraveling.

The lack of pattern wasn't just perplexing—it was dangerous. It meant the killer could strike anywhere, at any time, targeting anyone. No one was safe, and Atharva knew that unless he found a breakthrough soon, the city would descend into panic.

As the clock ticked toward midnight, Atharva stared out the window of his bungalow, the distant hum of Delhi's streets filling the silence. Somewhere out there, a killer was lurking—a shadow in the night, methodically planning their next move.

Atharva clenched his jaw, a surge of resolve flooding through him. "I'll find you," he whispered to the darkness. "No matter how deep you hide, I'll find you."

Unbeknownst to him, the case wasn't just a test of his skills—it was a test of his very soul.

Chapter 4

Time moved relentlessly, but the murders showed no sign of abating. Each new day brought fresh terror, a grim reminder of Atharva's growing inability to catch the shadowy killer. The weight of the case bore down on him, pressing harder with every unsolved crime. Sleep became a luxury, and his once-unwavering focus began to waver under the strain of unrelenting failure.

As New Year's Eve approached, Atharva's team urged him to take a break. "Sir, even you need a moment to breathe," one of his subordinates insisted. Atharva, initially resistant, eventually conceded. Perhaps a brief escape could provide the clarity he desperately needed.

He found himself in Goa that night, amidst the festive lights and pulsating energy of beachside celebrations. The sound of crashing waves mixed with laughter and music, creating an intoxicating atmosphere. For the first time in months, Atharva allowed himself to let go—just for a while.

It was at a party under the starlit sky that he saw her. She stood out from the crowd effortlessly, a woman in her late twenties, her laughter cutting through the noise like a melody. There was a natural elegance about her, a grace that made Atharva's gaze linger. He was captivated—not just by her beauty but by the warmth she radiated.

As the night unfolded, he found himself drawn to her, weaving through the crowd until they were close enough to speak. Her name was **Avni**, and she had a quick wit and an easy charm that made conversation flow effortlessly. For the first time in what felt like forever, Atharva wasn't thinking about crime scenes or unsolved murders. He was thinking about her.

By the time the clock struck 3 AM, he was tipsy—not just from the alcohol but from the way her presence had eased the storm in his mind. Mustering a boldness he didn't know he possessed, Atharva asked for her number. To his surprise and delight, she gave it to him with a teasing smile.

When he stumbled back to his hotel room, still feeling the buzz of the night, he laughed at himself. "What were you thinking, Atharva?" he muttered, shaking his head as he fell into bed. **"I must have been drunk on more than just the party... who knew I had the courage to ask an angel for**

her number? But, damn, was it worth it."

The next morning, however, the boldness of the night before left him reeling. He stared at his phone, Avni's number saved in it, and laughed nervously. "Oh shit, this is so embarrassing," he said aloud, rubbing his temples. But the thought of her—her laugh, her voice—nudged him past his hesitation. He texted her.

To his relief, she responded, and their conversation flowed as naturally as it had the night before. He learned that she was a psychiatrist, passionate about helping people untangle the complexities of their minds. Avni's work fascinated Atharva, and her ability to listen and understand resonated with him deeply.

The connection between them grew quickly, fueled by long calls and shared laughter. They decided to meet again, and when Atharva asked if she'd consider dating him, Avni said yes. The simplicity of her acceptance made his heart lighter, a feeling he hadn't experienced in years.

Though they lived in different cities, their bond deepened. Atharva found solace in her presence, even from afar. Back in Delhi, the murder case still loomed like a dark cloud over his days, but now, there was a ray of light cutting through the shadows. Avni became his confidante, the person he could share his thoughts with when the burden felt too heavy to bear.

Their relationship wasn't without its challenges—the distance, his erratic schedule, the all-consuming nature of his work—but they found ways to make it work. For the first time, Atharva felt as though he wasn't alone in his battles.

Yet, despite Avni's calming presence, the murders continued to haunt him. Every evening, as he sat in his dimly lit study, poring over evidence that refused to yield answers, the case gnawed at his mind. But now, when the weight became too much, he reached for his phone, and Avni's voice reminded him that he was more than the sum of his failures.

The killer was still out there, and the city's fear continued to grow, but Atharva knew one thing for certain: whatever lay ahead, he wouldn't face it alone.

Chapter 5

Atharva and Avni's marriage was the perfect blend of companionship and understanding. Their days were filled with laughter and shared dreams. Atharva, despite his intense job, always made time for Avni, and she, in turn, became his anchor in life's stormy seas. They often teased each other like old friends, finding joy in the smallest moments.

Once, during a lazy Sunday breakfast, Atharva tried to impress Avni by flipping pancakes like a pro, only to have one land on the floor. "Detective Atharva, you're better at catching criminals than catching pancakes," she teased, making him laugh until he was wiping away tears. Another time, Avni, not one to cook often, decided to surprise Atharva with a homemade dinner. The result was a slightly burnt, overly spicy meal, which Atharva ate with a straight face, declaring it "the finest cuisine ever" just to see her giggle.

Their camaraderie extended beyond their home. They played board games that often turned competitive, watched late-night crime thrillers (where Avni would humorously criticize his job, saying, "You'd solve it faster than the hero"), and even embarked on long drives where the silence was as comforting as their conversations.

Life was good—until Avni started noticing something unsettling about Atharva.

It began subtly, almost imperceptibly. At midnight, whenever the old grandfather clock in the living room chimed, Atharva would stir in his sleep. His expression would change, his features tightening as though in response to an invisible cue. At first, Avni thought it was a mere quirk, a restless sleeper reacting to a sound.

But it wasn't just restlessness. Over time, his reactions became more alarming. Atharva would wake suddenly, his movements stiff and his eyes distant, as though he wasn't entirely present. Without saying a word, he would get up, leave the house, and return hours later, slipping back into bed as though nothing had happened.

Avni tried to reason it out. Perhaps it was the stress of his work, the strain of unsolved cases weighing on him even in sleep. But the pattern continued, and his behavior grew stranger. He never remembered leaving when she asked him the next morning. "Are you sure you're not imagining it, Avni?" he'd say, laughing nervously.

One night, determined to get answers, Avni stayed awake. She watched as Atharva jolted upright when the clock struck twelve, his movements mechanical. He didn't even glance her way as he left the house. Fear and curiosity waged a battle within her, but she resolved to follow him the next time.

Something wasn't right. The man she knew so intimately was slipping into a version of himself she didn't recognize. Beneath his laughter and their shared happiness lay a shadowy secret—one that was beginning to unravel, piece by chilling piece.

Atharva's midnight episodes had become a disturbing and repetitive pattern. Every night, when the grandfather clock struck twelve, something inside him would shift. He would wake with a vacant, almost disconnected look in his eyes, leave the house without a word, and return hours later, as if nothing had happened. The most unsettling part was that he had no memory of his actions.

At first, Avni tried to dismiss it as simple stress. Being married to a high-ranking police officer came with its own pressures, and she knew how hard Atharva worked. But as a psychiatrist, Avni couldn't ignore the subtle shifts in his behavior that went beyond normal work fatigue. There was something more to his condition—something that wasn't just about the weight of his cases.

For weeks, Avni carefully observed him. His behavior during the day had started to change too—slight irritability, vague memories of events, and moments when his sharp intellect seemed to slip, even if only for a brief moment. She began to note the small details. The midnight episodes were always triggered by the chiming of the clock, and when he returned, he appeared completely unaware of the hours he'd spent outside. It was as though another person had taken over his body during those late hours.

As a psychiatrist, Avni had worked with various mental health conditions, but this was different. It was personal. She knew she had to understand what was happening to Atharva, not just for his well-being but for their future together.

Her training told her that such a pattern could indicate Dissociative Identity Disorder (DID)—a condition where a person's psyche splits into separate identities or personalities, often in response to deep, unresolved trauma. The episodes Atharva experienced, his amnesia, and the strange shift in his personality at night all fit the symptoms of DID.

But diagnosing Atharva, especially when he was her husband, was no easy task. She struggled with the thought of confronting him about it. Could she, as his wife, tell him he was suffering from something so profound? Could she ask him to face a part of himself he was likely unaware of? She understood the complexities of DID, but that didn't make it easier to reconcile with the man she loved.

Avni decided to carefully observe his behavior before jumping to any conclusions. She started tracking the times of his episodes more systematically. She kept a journal, recording his mood swings, the words he spoke, and the way his behavior shifted during and after the episodes. It wasn't easy; each entry deepened her concern. Every time she saw him return from one of those midnight walks, disoriented and confused, her heart broke just a little more.

Over the course of several weeks, Avni became increasingly certain. Atharva was suffering from DID. It was an overwhelming realization, but it was also a crucial step toward understanding how to help him. She knew that DID wasn't something that could be fixed overnight, and Atharva had to come to terms with it in his own time. For now, the only thing she could do was support him—without alarming him.

The hardest part was maintaining her composure. As a psychiatrist, she had the knowledge, but as his wife, she felt helpless. She couldn't bear to see the man she loved struggling with something so profound, especially when he didn't even know it was happening.

Her commitment to him, however, only grew stronger. Avni decided to take small steps to help Atharva regain control over his life. She gently encouraged him to talk about his feelings, to address the stresses of his work in a more open way. They had long conversations, sometimes late at night, about his childhood, his fears, and the burdens he carried. It was slow progress, but Avni hoped that by bringing these suppressed emotions to the surface, she could help him regain control over his fragmented mind.

Despite the weight of her secret, Avni knew one thing for sure—she wouldn't give up on him. She was his ally, his guide, and even if he couldn't see it yet, she would do everything she could to help him heal. After all, she was his wife, and that meant

*fighting for him in ways he couldn't
yet understand.*

Chapter 6

Avni, being a psychiatrist, couldn't ignore the signs. Each time the grandfather clock struck twelve, he would wake up, his expression blank and distant, as though he wasn't entirely present. He'd leave the house in a trance-like state, only to return hours later with no memory of where he had been or what he had done.

At first, she assumed it was work stress. Atharva's role as a top-ranking police officer came with enormous pressure, and she had seen how cases consumed him. But this was different—far beyond the typical burnout she had encountered in her professional life. It was as if a part of him switched off, leaving behind someone else entirely.

As both his wife and a mental health professional, Avni felt conflicted. On one hand, she loved Atharva deeply and didn't want to overstep the boundaries of their relationship by analyzing him clinically. On the other hand, her instincts as a psychiatrist told her this behavior wasn't normal. She began observing him closely, noting the details of his episodes and his behavior during the day.

Over time, a disturbing pattern emerged. His demeanor would shift subtly but unmistakably—moments of uncharacteristic irritability, unexplained exhaustion, and gaps in his usually sharp memory. During conversations, he sometimes seemed distracted, as if his mind was elsewhere. Avni knew these signs pointed to something serious, and her professional curiosity soon turned into concern.

She decided to approach the issue delicately, not wanting to alarm Atharva. Using her expertise, she began initiating subtle, therapeutic conversations, asking about his stress levels, his sleep patterns, and any recurring dreams or thoughts. She framed these discussions as casual talks between a husband and wife, but in reality, she was carefully assessing his mental state.

After several of these "sessions," the pieces began to fall into place. Avni realized that Atharva's episodes were more than stress-related—they were symptomatic of a deeper psychological condition. His midnight awakenings, his lack of memory, and his altered behavior all pointed to Dissociative Identity Disorder (DID).

The revelation shook her to the core. Atharva wasn't just her husband—he was a man grappling with an internal struggle he didn't even recognize. His mind had created an alternate identity, likely triggered by suppressed trauma, and that identity was taking control during the midnight episodes.

As a psychiatrist, Avni understood the complexities of DID, but as a wife, the discovery was heartbreaking. She knew confronting Atharva directly could be dangerous, both emotionally and mentally, so she resolved to proceed with caution.

Avni began documenting everything—his triggers, his behavior before and after the episodes, and any changes she noticed in his daily life. She started subtly guiding him toward moments of self-reflection, hoping he might begin to recognize the gaps in his memory and the shifts in his behavior.

Her nights became sleepless, not just because of Atharva's episodes but because of the weight of her knowledge. She felt a profound responsibility to help him, both as his wife and as a professional. But the dual role she played made the situation even more complicated.

Despite her growing fears, Avni's determination never wavered. She had seen countless patients face their demons and come out stronger. She believed Atharva could, too—but only if she approached the situation with care and precision.

Each midnight chime of the clock became a reminder of her mission. Atharva wasn't just the man she loved—he was someone in need of help, someone she was determined to save, even if it meant uncovering the darkest corners of his mind.

Chapter 7

Avni had tried everything. She had approached the situation with care and dedication, driven by love and a deep sense of responsibility. But despite her best efforts, Atharva's condition seemed insurmountable. The midnight episodes grew more frequent, the murders more brutal. Each time the grandfather clock chimed, the transformation occurred—Atharva would leave the house, his actions entirely driven by the alternate persona that had taken hold of him. And in his wake, death followed.

Over time, the consequences of his disorder became undeniable. There were more than 2,000 deaths—murders, to be precise—committed by the very man who was supposed to be the protector of the city. The statistics were staggering, each victim adding to the unending list of the innocent lives lost in the wake of Atharva's fractured mind.

Avni's heart ached every time she witnessed the disconnect between the man she had married and the one who was causing so much destruction. She had tried everything to help him—medications, therapy, and countless sleepless nights spent watching over him. But each time she thought they had made progress, the darkness would return. The alternate identity within Atharva was relentless, as if it thrived on his pain and suppressed memories.

Her love for him had once been the guiding force behind everything she did. She had believed that if she could just reach him, if she could just break through the walls of his mind, she could save him. But the more time passed, the clearer it became that Atharva's DID wasn't just a personal battle anymore. It was a public danger—one that was beyond her control.

One evening, as she sat alone in the dim light of their living room, staring at the clock ticking in the corner, a chilling realization washed over her. Atharva was no longer just a man struggling with his past. He was a weapon—an unstoppable force of chaos—and the longer she let him spiral, the more lives would be lost. The toll had become too great, and the city had already suffered irreparably.

Avni had always believed that love could heal anything. She had hoped that by standing by Atharva, by supporting him, she could fix what had been broken. But now, as the weight of his crimes pressed down on her, she realized that she could no longer afford to be blinded by her love. Her first responsibility was to the people—to the lives that continued to be taken by the very person who had once been their protector.

The final straw came when she received another call, another body, another victim. As her eyes scanned the chilling details of the murder, a cold realization seized her heart. The police couldn't stop it. No one could. Atharva's dual identity was a time bomb, ticking away with each passing second. It was only a matter of time before he claimed even more lives. No amount of love, no amount of effort, could change what he had become.

In that moment, the weight of her decision settled over her like a suffocating fog. Avni knew what she had to do. She couldn't save Atharva anymore—not the man he was now. The city needed her. The people needed her to act, to stop the madness before it spiraled even further.

With a heavy heart and a mind clouded by anguish, Avni made a choice—she would save the city, even if it meant sacrificing the love of her life. She would do whatever it took to stop the killings, even if it meant

confronting the terrifying truth that
Atharva, the man she had loved so
deeply, had become the very monster
she had once tried to protect him
from.

In the end, love wasn't enough to heal
him. And with the city's future at
stake, Avni was ready to face the
hardest truth of all: sometimes, the
one you love most is the one you must
let go of, in order to save everyone
else.

Chapter 8

Avni's heart was heavy as she looked at Atharva across the room. He was so unaware of what was coming, so lost in his own world, still so charming in his naivety. Their marriage had been full of love, laughter, and countless beautiful moments, but now, it felt like she was watching the life they built together slowly unravel.

She knew what needed to be done. There was no way around it anymore. Atharva's DID had destroyed not just him but so many innocent lives. His nightly transformation, his unconscious killings, had gone on for far too long. But he was still the man she had married—the man she had fallen in love with. And this love, this haunting connection, was now a source of unbearable grief for her.

She stared at the photograph of them on their wedding day, smiling, radiant, full of hope. And now, the very man she had pledged to stand by was a threat to everything around them. The clock ticking in the background echoed in her mind like a constant reminder of the ticking time bomb they were living with.

And so, she decided. If she couldn't save him, if she couldn't help him break free from this fractured reality, then she would save the city. And she would do it with the last remaining shred of love she had left in her.

She asked him to go on a date with her—to Paris, a city they had always dreamed of visiting together. He agreed with his usual enthusiasm, unaware that this would be their last trip.

The trip to Paris was both a dream and a nightmare.

The Eiffel Tower loomed over them as they strolled through the cobbled streets of Montmartre, the evening air cool and fragrant with the scent of freshly baked bread. Atharva's laughter was infectious, and for a moment, Avni was able to forget the darkness closing in on them.

They ate dinner in a quaint café, and Atharva, ever the charmer, spoke animatedly about the case he had been working on before they left. His eyes sparkled with excitement, and Avni smiled softly, masking the sorrow in her heart. The man she loved was still in there, somewhere, but she knew deep down that he was already lost to her.

As they walked through the narrow streets, Avni remembered the quiet moments they'd shared in the past—the way he would hold her hand with such tenderness, the way they would laugh over simple things, the way he would look at her as though she was his world. But those moments felt distant now, as if they belonged to another lifetime, another reality.

And then there were the moments when she caught glimpses of the man she once knew. He would pause, his face contorting in confusion, as if something inside him was breaking apart. For those fleeting seconds, she could almost see the desperation in his eyes, a silent plea for her to save him. But she couldn't.

Finally, as they reached a quiet, deserted alleyway near the Seine, the moment she had dreaded arrived. Atharva stood with his back to her, gazing at the distant city lights, completely unaware of the danger. She stood behind him, her heart aching, her hands trembling.

This was it. The culmination of everything they had been through. It had to be done.

Avni pulled out the gun, her hands shaking violently. She took a deep breath, trying to steady herself, but nothing could calm the storm inside her. She walked quietly up behind him, her footsteps barely making a sound on the cobblestone. Her heart pounded in her chest as she raised the weapon, her eyes locking on the back of his head.

She couldn't help but remember the man he had once been—the man who had promised to love her forever, the man who had held her hand as they stepped into the future together. But now, that man is gone. The man who stood before her was a stranger—one she loved, yet one who had become a monster. And with that thought, she pulled the trigger.

The sound of the shot echoed through the still night, and Atharva crumpled to the ground, lifeless.

Avni stood frozen, staring at the body of the man she had loved, the man who had once been her entire world. Her tears fell freely now, uncontrollable and bitter.

"I'm sorry, Atharva," she whispered, her voice breaking. "I couldn't save you. But I couldn't let you hurt anyone else either."

She knelt beside him, gently brushing his hair from his face, her fingers trembling. "I wish... I wish you could have been the man I married. I wish I could have saved you from the darkness inside you. But now, all I can do is let you rest."

Her sobs echoed in the empty alley, the weight of her decision crushing her spirit. She had chosen to end his life, not out of hatred, but out of love—the kind of love that could not allow more innocent lives to be lost.

She kissed his forehead one final time, a farewell that would haunt her for the rest of her life.

"I'll always love you," she whispered softly, the words carrying the weight of her grief.

And with that, she turned away, leaving Paris, leaving the man she once loved, to fade into the past—a painful memory she would never forget.

Epilogue
And with that the unseen other was seen by the closet one of the actual seen.

I wish someday walking through the streets, I would find a copy of this book somewhere in the market, being sold, to some Avni, who is willing to lose her beloved to save others. but somewhere deep down i know i will never be Avni, i would let 100 unseen people die rather than losing the one i love.

At the end I would like to thank y'all for reading these pages.
grateful.

-garvita
(not so avni)